THE S.

Imagine if you had to te   , ᴛo save
their life. Imagine if yo   , came magically
alive, itself. This is what happens to Barbara in
The Snow Door.

Charles Ashton has spent most of his life in
Scotland. He now lives in the village where he
was brought up and his two youngest children go
to the school that he went to. His books for
young people include *Jet Smoke and Dragon Fire*
(shortlisted for both the Guardian Fiction Award
and the WH Smith Mind Boggling Books Award)
and three stories for younger readers, *Ruth and
the Blue Horse*, *The Giant's Boot* (shortlisted for
the 1995 Smarties Book Prize) and *The Boy Who
Was a Bear*.

Books by the same author

The Boy Who Was a Bear

The Giant's Boot

Ruth and the Blue Horse

For older readers

Billy's Drift

The Dragon Fire Trilogy

❧ THE ❧
SNOW DOOR

CHARLES ASHTON
Illustrations by
PETER MELNYCZUK

WALKER BOOKS
AND SUBSIDIARIES
LONDON • BOSTON • SYDNEY

*This book is dedicated to all those involved in
the Young Authors Project in Dundee and
with thanks to my aunt, Mary Dryburgh,
who first prodded the man in the snow.*

C.A.

First published 1998 by Walker Books Ltd
87 Vauxhall Walk, London SE11 5HJ

This edition published 1999

2 4 6 8 10 9 7 5 3 1

This book has been typeset in Plantin.

Printed in England by Clays Ltd, St Ives plc

British Library Cataloguing in Publication Data
A catalogue record for this book
is available from the British Library.

ISBN 0-7445-6958-3

Contents

Chapter One 7

Chapter Two 15

Chapter Three....................................25

Chapter Four....................................39

Chapter Five....................................51

Chapter Six 59

Chapter Seven 71

Chapter Eight....................................83

Chapter One

Chapter One

···

The sky was not blue like ours, but pink. And the trees were like rainbow feathers, and the birds called in sweet voices like clarinets. Sherry-Sad stepped through the magic doorway onto a narrow path between golden rocks. It led downhill, sometimes down flights of slippery steps, towards the distant valley.

Sherry-Sad would have spent longer in looking and listening to all the wonderful things in the strange land, but she knew she must hurry, because down in the valley was the thing she really wanted. However, she did stop to lick the golden rocks, because they looked so smooth and glass-like. They tasted like sugar-candy, only not quite so sweet.

Barbara closed her secret notebook. She had reached page ten of her story. She smiled, thinking of her lickable rocks. She didn't like sugar-candy much herself because it was too sweet. For most of the years when the War was on she had had hardly any sweets. Now that there were more to be had, she found she didn't enjoy them as much as she remembered doing before.

The train had not yet reached the big bridge over the Tay, which was when she normally put her notebook away, but she had reached the difficult part in her story. This part was so difficult she might even have to give up.

Barbara didn't always manage to write when she was on the train on the way to school, but she had managed to avoid Miss English today.

She didn't mind Miss English, but conversation with her was a bit limited, as the only things the teacher ever wanted to know were how Barbara was getting on at school, and how many sums had she done the day before and when was her next spelling test and was she looking forward to learning French and Latin when she got to the upper school.

Miss English taught in the upper school, and she and Barbara were the only two people in St Syras who went to the school in Dundee. In the mornings they had to get there with the half-past-seven bus to Stratheden, then the eight o'clock train.

Barbara would manage to avoid Miss English perhaps three times a week, and that was when she would sit and dream and hum to herself and make up stories. On the other two days Miss English would see her and talk to her, and she had to be polite and try to think of things to say.

Barbara often wished she could still go to the village school with the other boys and girls who had always been her friends. But her mother had told her that Uncle Hugh would have wanted her to have the best possible education, and that was why Barbara had to be sent to an especially good and expensive school.

Uncle Hugh was her mother's brother, and he had been killed in the Second World War. He had been fighting against the Japanese in Burma. It turned out that Uncle Hugh had quite a lot of money, and he left it all to Barbara's mother. Barbara's mother had decided that the money should be used to send Barbara to the expensive school.

Barbara did remember Uncle Hugh a little, but it was four years since she had seen him. On that occasion he had taken her into the garden to play football and had pretended to slip on the ball and then really had slipped and fallen into the flower-bed and flattened her father's asters. Her mother had scolded Uncle Hugh terribly but he had simply stuck out his tongue at her.

Barbara didn't think Uncle Hugh seemed the kind of uncle who would want her to be taken away from all her friends at the village school and made to go off to Dundee so early in the morning; but her mother and father both said it was what Uncle Hugh would have wanted and Barbara supposed they would know better than she.

It was because of Uncle Hugh that she had given the heroine of her story such a peculiar name, Sherry-Sad. Ever since Uncle Hugh had been killed her mother would have bouts of sadness; and when one of these bouts came on she would go to the sideboard in the dining-room and pour herself a glass of sherry. Barbara disapproved of this, because the sherry seemed to make her even sadder, but, her mother told her, it was "a nice kind of sadness – a sweet kind"; so that was how Barbara had thought up the name.

Barbara's present story was called "The Pleasant Land", and it was written in rather wobbly writing because it was difficult to write neatly on the moving train. It had seemed like a good title to begin with, because writing the story had been very pleasant too. But the nearer things got to that one difficult part, the slower Barbara had become. Now she had reached it at last and she could no longer avoid the difficulty.

The train clanked its way slowly towards Dundee, and Sherry-Sad made her way slowly down to the Pleasant Land; but although Barbara expected that she herself would get to Dundee both on this and on many other mornings, she wasn't at all sure that Sherry-Sad would ever reach her valley: and that was because of the person who was waiting for her there.

Chapter Two

Chapter Two

The only thing wrong with Miss English was having to talk with her all the way to Dundee. Apart from that she was perfectly all right. And there was something that made it worthwhile being polite to her: she was a keen skier, and the year before had offered to take Barbara up to Glen Shee at weekends and give her lessons.

By the time the snows had melted at the end of that winter Barbara had become fairly good on the gentler slopes. Her heavy black skis kept her firmly on the ground and as long as she kept them both pointing in the same direction she didn't have much to worry about. But what she liked best was cross-country skiing. It was even better than riding a bicycle, because you felt as if you were walking and yet it was so effortless and fast.

The winter after the one when she first learned to ski – the winter when she started her story about Sherry-Sad, the winter of 1947 – turned out to be the worst anyone could remember. It was unusually mild in January, but then suddenly the weather changed and back it came – winter wild as the North Pole, with endless blizzards and hard frosts and the road continually getting blocked for days on end. Barbara was able to ski every single weekend, though she never got the chance to go to Glen Shee.

Whenever the road over the hill to Stratheden got blocked, it meant the bus couldn't get through, and that meant that there was no school. After this had happened a few times Miss English called one Monday and said she had heard that the snow wasn't too bad on the Stratheden side of the hill and the trains were still running.

"I think," she said to Barbara, "that we should get our skis on and ski over to Stratheden and catch the train from there tomorrow. What do you think?"

And of course Barbara could hardly say "No, I'd rather get my skis on and ski about St Syras all day," though that was what she would have liked to have said.

In the first light of the winter morning the only colour was blue, a dim, formless, misty blue that was both spooky and beautiful. Everything was hummocked in soft rounded shapes: nothing could be recognized under the thick silvery blanket. Barbara had almost forgotten what the real countryside around her home looked like anyway.

Barbara and Miss English headed uphill, straight across country. They laughed to think that the snow was so deep they could be going straight over the top of fences and hedges and never know it, but then Miss English reminded her that she should concentrate on her skiing so that they didn't lose time; and after that they went in silence, Barbara watching the pale mist of her breath, which seemed to be the only thing that was moving, and listening to the lovely *swish-swish-swish* of their skis on the snow, which was the only sound to be heard. This would be something to tell them at school, at least!

Suddenly Miss English stopped and stood looking down at the point of her ski-stick. Barbara halted too.

"That's most peculiar," Miss English said, and lifted her stick slightly, then dropped the point into the snow again. There was a sound: not exactly enough of a sound to be anything you could recognize, but more of a sound than the point of the stick normally made in the snow, and – "Look there," Miss English said, now scraping at the snow with her stick until through it a colour suddenly appeared: a small streak of dark red…

"Good gracious," Miss English said, and then looked up, first up the hill and then down the hill, as if trying to work something out. "This must be the road."

The first thing Barbara thought was that it couldn't possibly be the road because the road wasn't red. Then she realized that of course the road must be buried much farther down beneath the snow than this red thing. By the time it had dawned on her what Miss English meant, the teacher was bending down and busily digging the snow away with her woolly mittens. More and more red appeared, a smooth, shiny, flat red surface.

"Good gracious," Miss English said again. Then, "I know what this is: it's the mail-van. It must have got stuck here in the early hours and – oh, good gracious."

The third good gracious sounded pretty serious, though Barbara couldn't particularly think why. Then Miss English started clearing more snow away from the mail-van roof and then digging a hole down into the snow at one corner. Then she unbuckled her skis and lay down on the roof with her head in the hole she had made. Barbara wondered if the snow had made Miss English go mad.

After hanging her head in the snow hole for a few minutes and occasionally throwing up more handfuls of snow, Miss English raised herself onto her knees and turned to Barbara and said, "Well, thank goodness for that: there's no one there, he must have got away." Then at last Barbara realized that the postman could have been trapped in his van, and buried under all the snow.

"He might have got frozen," she said.

"That's what I was worried about," Miss English said. "I just hope he found his way to the houses. Come on, we'll miss our train if we don't hurry."

They continued their journey. But something seemed to have changed. The snowy world no longer seemed quite so fresh and exciting and adventurous. Barbara glanced back once and saw the dark splash of red in the snow where the mail van was. It looked dirty somehow, and sinister, like a bloodstain.

They reached the brow of the hill. Snowy

land stretched away to the horizons. Ahead of them lay the sea, looking like lead under the blue-grey sky. They passed a lonely hawthorn tree, bare and mournful, and had just begun to pick up speed when Miss English gave an exclamation and swished off to the right in a sharp curve.

Barbara got mixed up between meaning to follow Miss English and meaning to stop, and her skis crossed and she fell over. By the time she had picked herself up and rearranged herself, she saw Miss English had stopped and was bending over a dark something in the snow. Quickly she went over to join her.

Chapter Three

Chapter Three

In a shallow scoop hollowed in the snow a man was lying. He was wearing an ordinary long grey coat and black wellingtons and woollen gloves, but on his head there was a flat black postman's cap. The man's face looked blue-grey and his eyes were closed, but it seemed he had just said something to Miss English.

"But what were you thinking of? What were you trying to do?" Miss English immediately demanded, in a terrifyingly teacherish voice. Barbara wondered that the postman didn't leap to his feet and stand to attention at the very sound of it.

Instead he muttered – he seemed to be quite an old man, with grey hair in his moustache – "Try to get to Stratheden... Get warm..."

"I know you wanted to get warm," Miss English said indignantly, "but why in heaven's name didn't you just go on down to St Syras? You were almost there! Stratheden's miles away."

"St Syras..." the old postman mumbled. "'Sright. Couldn't see... Have to get to Stratheden..."

"He must have got lost in the blowing snow," Miss English remarked to Barbara. "Probably couldn't tell if he was going uphill or downhill."

"What are we going to do?" Barbara asked. She felt scared. She didn't know how long the man had been out in the snow, but she knew it was possible to freeze to death in this kind of weather.

"You have to get up," Miss English said in a loud, clear voice. "You can't stay there. Can you get up?"

"Get up," the old postman repeated. He seemed to be drowsy and he didn't open his eyes when he spoke. "Get to Stratheden. You go on, I'll have a little rest."

"No," Miss English said. "You can't have a little rest. You'll die if you stay there. You have to get up." And she prodded him sharply with her ski-stick.

At that the man opened his eyes. He looked bleary and bewildered but the prod seemed to have done him some good. "Hey!" he said. "That's enough of that! Just you get on your way, I'm doing fine here."

"You're doing nothing of the kind," Miss English retorted. "And I want you up on your feet this instant."

Barbara cringed. Was this what it was going to be like when she was in Miss English's class?

But the postman was undaunted. "Away you go, woman," he said angrily. "Get on your road and leave me be. I'm having five minutes of a rest and that's the end of it."

"Very well," Miss English said, and turned away.

"Are we just going to leave him here?"

Barbara asked, surprised that Miss English seemed to have changed her mind so quickly. "Will he be all right?"

"No, of course he won't," Miss English said in a slightly lower voice. "But I don't think we can move him. So this is what we're going to have to do. I'll go back to St Syras and get help, but in the meantime I want you to stay here with him and keep him talking."

"What, me?" Barbara felt horrified at the thought. "But he's such a crosspatch – and he doesn't want anyone talking to him."

"It doesn't matter," Miss English said severely. "It's a typical symptom. He's not himself, he's just talking unreasonably. It doesn't matter what he says, what you have to do is stop him from falling asleep. He wants to fall asleep, you see, but if he does he might never wake up again. Do you understand?"

Barbara nodded dumbly. She wanted to argue – if it had been her mother, she would have argued – but she didn't think she ought to argue with Miss English. And anyway, what Miss English said was probably right. "B-but what if he just falls asleep?" she stammered. "What if I can't make him stay awake?"

"You've just got to try," Miss English answered. "Poke him, kick him, do anything you like. It doesn't matter about being polite. It's much more important to make sure he stays alive. Now I must hurry – I'll be as quick as I can."

And she was off, *swish-swish*ing through the snow back the way they had come.

"But – " Barbara said in a tiny squeak of a voice that even the postman couldn't have heard, let alone Miss English. She watched the teacher dwindling into the distance, passing the bare hawthorn tree and disappearing from view. Slowly she turned to the man.

His eyes were closed again. That was bad. Barbara gave a little cough. Perhaps that would make him stir.

It didn't. She cleared her throat again.

"Em – my name's Barbara," she tried, nothing like loud enough. She was going to die of embarrassment.

It was no use. The postman's eyes were still shut. She was going to have to do something. She took her skis off and went over and kicked him. He jerked, and his eyes popped open again. "Who the devil are you?" he growled.

"I'm Barbara," Barbara said. "I'm sorry, I didn't mean to kick you hard. Miss English said I had to keep you awake."

"Is that what they teach you young things nowadays?" the postman said, raising himself slightly on his elbow. "Kick old men when they're down? I don't know what the world's coming to."

"Just – please don't fall asleep again," Barbara said. "Miss English's gone for help, but she says you've got to stay awake and that's why she said I had to stay with you. You see?"

"She your teacher, that old bat?"

Barbara giggled. "She teaches at my school. She's not exactly my teacher."

"Well, I'm from Dundee myself," the postman said.

That seemed a queer thing to say, but it gave Barbara an idea what she could talk about. "That's where I go to school," she said brightly. "Dundee."

"And what's wrong with St Syras school?" the man demanded angrily.

Barbara sighed. "Nothing. I used to go there. But my mother wants me to go to school in Dundee now."

The old postman sank down into a lying position again and his eyes flickered. Barbara thought desperately of a way to continue the conversation. "It's a long way to school," she said. "That's why we've got to start so early. And the train journey can be boring, but – but I while away the time by writing stories…"

He was listening. "Stories, eh?" he said. "What kind of stories?"

"Well –" Barbara said. It didn't matter what she said to him, as long as she stopped him from falling asleep. She could even tell him her story. "Well," she said, "at the present moment I'm writing a story called 'The Pleasant Land'."

"'The Pleasant Land,' eh?" the old postman chuckled. "That was where I was going – before you came along and started poking me. The Pleasant Land."

"It wouldn't have been pleasant if you'd fallen asleep," Barbara told him. "You'd have died…" But then she stopped, and wondered if she had said something stupid. Everyone said that when you died you went to Heaven, and she supposed that Heaven was a kind of Pleasant Land too. She decided to go on with her story. "It's about a girl called Sherry-Sad, who—"

"Sherry what? Who called her that? That's a daft name for a girl."

Barbara shrivelled with embarrassment. He was right, it was a terrible name. She would alter that. "Oh," she said, "did I say Sherry-Sad? I didn't mean that. Her real name is – em – Barbarella."

"Bar-bar-ella!" the old postman exploded. "That's even dafter. I'm not listening to any story about someone called Barbarella. I liked Sherry-Sack. It's a nice name."

"All right then," Barbara said, "I'll call her Sherry-Sad. Just for you." But she told herself she would change it as soon as she got home.

"Sherry-Sack, then," the old man growled. "Barbarella, indeed! Get on with it then, let's hear your story."

"Well, this girl called Sherry-Sad," Barbara went on, "is an only child, but she doesn't want to be, because she wants a brother."

"A brother!" the old postman broke in again. "What does she want a brother for?"

Barbara bit her lip. Was this what the whole story was going to be like? Nothing but interruptions? What was wrong with Sherry-Sad wanting a brother? Again she felt embarrassed. Perhaps good storytellers didn't tell stories about girls who wanted brothers. It wasn't fair. She had thought it was a good idea. She could change the name Sherry-Sad, but she could hardly change the story so that Sherry-Sad wasn't looking for a brother! She wished she hadn't started telling the old man her story at all.

She took a deep breath. "I don't know," she said. "She was lonely. It's just what the story is. It's just a story, you know."

"A daft story if you ask me," the old man said. "A girl wanting a brother. Girls don't want brothers. No, no. Never a little brother." He shook his head and closed his eyes.

"No!" Barbara screamed. "You mustn't close your eyes! You'll fall asleep!"

The old man's eyes popped open again and glared at her. "I wasn't falling asleep," he grunted crossly. "I could hardly fall asleep with you jabbering away at me. I was thinking."

"I'm sorry," Barbara said. "I was just doing what Miss English told me."

The old postman grunted again, this time with a little smile. "You're all right, my lass," he said more gently. "You just tell me your story. But why your Sherry-Sack wants a little brother I can't begin to think. She'd only hate him, that's for sure."

This intrigued Barbara. "Why is it so sure?" she asked him.

"I had a sister," the old man announced in a low voice.

Chapter Four

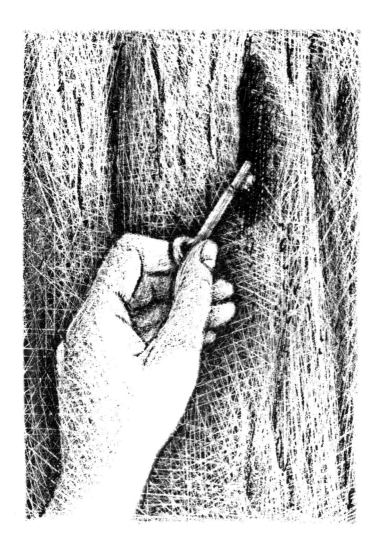

Chapter Four

Barbara felt surprised. She hadn't somehow thought of old men having sisters. "I didn't know you had a sister," she said.

"Of course you didn't," the old man snapped. "You've only just met me! Yes, I had a sister, and I can tell you we didn't get along."

"Why not?" Barbara asked.

The old postman grunted. "What do I know? She didn't like me. She thought I was stupid. She said all boys are dirty and stupid." He gave a little snort of laughter. "Maybe she was right. Boys grow up and they go to war and they kill a heap of other young chaps they don't even know. She was likely right. Likely we're all stupid."

"Were you in the War?" Barbara asked him.

"Not this war," he answered. "The Great War, I was in. From 1915 to 1917. I was at the Somme, have you heard of it?"

Barbara shook her head.

He snorted softly. "It was a battle, it doesn't matter. Do you know what it was like? Think of walking through the mud while someone's running red-hot pokers – *zip! zip!* – either side of your ears: that's the bullets from the enemy guns, and your friends are falling down on either side of you, but you have to keep on walking in case anyone thinks you're scared. That's it, you see, mud and guns: dirty and stupid. She's dead now, Elizabeth."

This left Barbara feeling a little bewildered. "Was Elizabeth your sister?" she asked.

The old postman nodded. "Betty, we called her. Sweaty Betty, I called her. I thought she deserved it. I don't now though."

"Was she killed in the War?" Barbara asked.

"No, not Betty," he chuckled. "There was an epidemic after the War. They called it the Spanish flu. That's what carried her off. Nigh-on thirty years ago now." He paused.

"That's terribly sad," Barbara said.

"No, no, you don't understand," the old postman broke in. He didn't seem at all drowsy now, but almost excited. "You see, there was something I'd always wanted to tell her. I'd played a terrible trick on her, long ago…"

Barbara waited. She had been going to tell him a story, and now it seemed he was going to tell her one instead! She felt quite relieved.

"We didn't live in Dundee at the time," he went on. "Oh, this was long ago, back in the 'nineties – the eighteen nineties, that is. We lived in a village. And there was a little wood, down beyond the end of my mother's washing-green.

"My sister was fond of animals, and she had a pet squirrel. No, not a pet: it was wild, but it would come to a box our father had put up in a tree, and Betty had trained this squirrel to come and eat out of her hand.

"I had a little Jack Russell terrier, Floss. I used to hunt rabbits with her. One day Floss came to me carrying a dead squirrel. I don't know if she'd killed it or if she'd just found it dead. I knew it wasn't Betty's squirrel, because we were a couple of miles away from home, but I thought of this trick I would play on her.

"I went home and I chucked the dead squirrel down on the green and went into the house. I told Betty: 'Floss has killed your squirrel.'

"She didn't believe me at first, but then I told her it was lying dead on the green, and she went and looked and – oh, you should have seen her face. Up to then I'd thought my trick had been a great success, but when I saw her face I thought maybe I'd gone too far.

"I'd thought she would go down into the wood and check if I was really telling the truth. But she didn't; I don't know why. So in the end I told her I'd been pulling her leg and her own squirrel was just fine. But, you see, she didn't believe me."

"Why ever not?" Barbara burst in.

"I don't know," he said. "I don't understand it. Maybe she thought it was another trick. I don't know. All I know is she never went to check. She never went beyond the washing-green again.

"My father got a job at the mills just after that and we moved into Dundee. Elizabeth never had another pet.

"Well, we grew up and then the War came, and off the boys marched to the Front. She was good to me then: she wrote me letters all the time I was away. Getting a letter from home was a wonderful thing when you were a young chap at the Front. It would remind you of good things, and you needed that when you were living there amongst the mud and the dead bodies for month after month.

"Well, I was wounded, and she moved to Wales, and somehow I never got the chance to speak to her before she died."

"Couldn't you have written to her?" Barbara asked. "Couldn't you have told her in a letter?"

"I was never a great one for writing letters," he replied. "Oh, the dominie taught us to read and write at the school, sure enough – many's the time I got his ruler across my knuckles when I hadn't formed a capital *A* or a capital *M* properly! I could write beautifully, but I just never seemed to know what to say in a letter. I took to delivering other people's letters instead, and here I am."

Barbara sighed. She had forgotten all about her own story. Her mind was racing as she tried to think of things the old man could have done to put things right with his sister before it had become too late.

"So," – vaguely she heard him speaking again – "that's my story. Now it's your turn to tell me yours."

"What?" Barbara said, coming to herself. "I mean – pardon?"

"Your story," the postman said. "Your story about – what was she called, now? – Sherry-Sack." He chuckled. "Maybe she was different from Betty."

"Oh, yes," Barbara said, without much enthusiasm. "I don't think you'd find my story very interesting."

"Get away," the old postman said heartily. "Of course I want to hear it. Did she get a brother? How did she go about it?"

"Well, she got a brother, yes," Barbara stammered. "But not in the ordinary way, you see. She gets him – well, it's by magic really."

"Magic!" the postman repeated. "That's something I haven't seen a great deal of. How does she get him by magic?"

"Well," Barbara said slowly, "she gets a magic key." She was being very careful what she said now, in case the man started making objections again.

But the old postman didn't seem to be so grumpy any more. "A magic key, eh?" he said. "That might be some use, I daresay, if you could find a magic keyhole."

"Well, yes, that's exactly what she does

find," Barbara said excitedly. "She finds a magic keyhole, though to begin with she doesn't realize it's a keyhole. It's just a hole in a tree, you see, and it's quite by accident that she puts her key into it."

"By accident?" the postman said. "Some accident! How did she stick a magic key into a magic hole by accident?"

"By accident!" Barbara repeated firmly. She liked telling her story this way. Now that she had got past the embarrassment of talking about it and the stupid names, she was starting to remember that it was actually quite good: she had been right to like it. She had no need to be embarrassed.

"Her mother had a beautiful locket that Sherry-Sad really liked; and one day her mother let her borrow it, and Sherry-Sad went off by herself with the locket, and when she was alone she decided she liked it so much that she would hide it and then tell her mother she had lost it, though in fact she could still come back and find it in its hiding place whenever she wanted to. So she slipped it into this hole in the tree; but then she thought better of it and decided to take it back after all and just ask to borrow it again, as a good person should.

"But when she tried to get the locket back out of the hole in the tree, she found it had stuck fast. And because she didn't have anything else with her to try and hook it out with, she put her magic key into the hole. And lo and behold the tree split in half, and it was a door into another Land.

"The sky of this other Land was not blue like ours, but pink. And the trees were like rainbow feathers, and there were birds with nice voices."

"I like birds too," the old postman murmured.

"Sherry-Sad stepped through the magic doorway and found she was on a steep path between golden rocks that led down into the valley. She was delighted at how it all looked but she had to hurry because the important thing she was really looking for was down in the valley. And after she had gone a long way she came to the bottom and looked out from between the rocks and there, sitting on the grass – it was blue grass, by the way – she saw him."

But here she stopped, as she had so often stopped before. Because here her story was stuck. The boy who was to be Sherry-Sad's magic brother was sitting there with his back turned to her. She could see his hair, short and sleek and black like the seals' heads she saw every morning as the train crossed over the Tay Bridge.

She was stuck, and he was the problem. The story couldn't get finished until she had solved this problem, and the problem couldn't be solved.

Chapter Five

Chapter Five

The problem was Sherry-Sad's brother, who
didn't behave like a made-up character.
Whenever she trod the narrow path down
between the sugar-candy rocks into the
Pleasant Land, he was there waiting for her,
and he was as solid and real as if she had
known him all her life. *And he was Japanese.*

Barbara couldn't understand why he had to
be Japanese. Her mother had told her terrible
things about the Japanese, who had killed
Uncle Hugh. But she couldn't seem to do
anything about it: it was simply the way her
story was.

Barbara thought hard about what she
should do. Now that she had got going, she
wanted to tell the old postman the story
properly – indeed, she didn't think she'd be
able to change it, even if she wanted to – but
she was almost certain she would offend him
if she told him that Sherry-Sad's brother was

a Japanese boy. Everyone else she knew would have been offended, or angry, if she had told them that. That was why she had kept her story so carefully hidden.

She gazed away across the pure white landscape, where the single black hawthorn-tree marked the brow of the hill down to the village. What should she do? What should she tell him? She would have to hurry and make up her mind and get on with the story, or else the man would fall asleep and she might not be able to save him.

There were swimming blue shapes in front of her eyes from having stared too long at all the whiteness. She blinked slowly and turned her head back to her companion.

His eyes were shut.

"No, man, no!" she almost shrieked. "No, Postie! Wake up! You mustn't fall asleep!"

The old man's lids scarcely moved. Barbara leaned over and grabbed his arm and shook it as hard as she could. The postman's eyes half-opened and he smiled slightly. "What now, my lass?" he murmured. "Have we reached the Pleasant Land yet?"

"Yes, yes we've reached it," Barbara replied, still shaking him. "I told you, don't you remember? Oh, you haven't been listening, and what's the use? You're just going to fall asleep and there's nothing I can do and – well, the thing is, it's a very strange thing, but her brother's a Japanese boy!"

The words came blurting out almost as if it were someone else saying them. She didn't know if she had been trying to shock him awake or what, but she couldn't have stopped herself even if she had tried.

It seemed to work, but Barbara immediately wished it hadn't. The postman's eyes opened properly and he stared at her very hard, while a frown gathered darkly on his forehead. Barbara gulped.

"What's this you're saying?" he said in a low but strangely threatening voice. "A Japanese boy? Why? The Japanese are the enemy, child. What are you thinking of?"

"I know they're the enemy," Barbara said, though she was finding it difficult to speak because of the horrible sinking feeling in her stomach. "They killed my Uncle Hugh, you know." Her voice was wavering as if she was going to cry, though in fact she didn't feel like crying.

"They killed your Uncle Hugh!" he repeated, as if in disbelief. "And you want one of them to be your brother?"

"*He* didn't kill my Uncle Hugh," Barbara protested. "He's just young, he didn't kill anyone."

"That makes no difference!" the old man almost shouted. His face was beginning to look rather terrifying and his cheeks wobbled as he spoke. "What's wrong with him being a good Scots boy – or a Frenchman, if you must have a foreigner? The French were our friends!"

"I tried that!" Barbara wailed. It was true: she had tried first to make him a Highland boy with red hair and freckles; and then she had tried to make him a French boy with nice brown eyes and a blue beret on his head; she had even tried to make him a blond-haired, blue-eyed Polish boy who couldn't say any English words except "You like I keess your hand?" as Captain Rostforowski had said to her mother and made her father so cross.

But none of them worked: they simply wouldn't get into her story. Only Albert worked. She was almost sure that Albert was not a Japanese name, but right from the start he had insisted on being called Albert – and he had insisted on being Japanese. "I can't make him do what I want him to," she tried to explain. "I can't make him stop being Japanese."

"You're telling me nonsense," he said flatly. He was not the way he had been before when he had kept interrupting her. She could see he was very angry. "You're just a child, and you're telling me you can't change a made-up story! I've never heard such a thing. I won't hear any more. I've had enough, do you hear me?" And very deliberately, like a door slamming in her face, he closed his eyes.

That was when Barbara discovered that the feeling she had started to have was in fact the feeling of being very angry. She suddenly realized she had had enough of this rude old man who didn't care that she wanted to help him. She had begun to think he was nice when he had told his story, but now she thought that the cruel trick he had played on his sister simply showed what he was really like: he was simply nasty, and didn't deserve to be helped.

"Right," Barbara said, turning from him and stumbling back to her skis. "Right." She stepped into them, buckled them, straightened up and seized her sticks which were standing upright in the snow. "Right." And she pushed off, *swish*, without another glance at him, downhill.

Chapter Six

Chapter Six

Almost as soon as she had pushed off,
Barbara slowed herself and stopped. She
couldn't do this. She had been told to look
after the old man and keep him awake and
she couldn't leave him, however cross he
made her. She turned back.

But oh, he seemed far away; and she
seemed to have forgotten how to ski uphill!
He wasn't so far away that she couldn't have
called to him, and perhaps let him know she
was coming and not to go to sleep; but she
was still a little too cross to do that. So she
heaved with her sticks and floundered with
her skis, but somehow couldn't make herself
move up the gentle slope towards him. She
even began to think she was slipping
backwards.

She unbuckled the skis and took them off
again, then gathered them and the sticks
under her arm and started to walk. One

step – two steps – she took. Luckily the snow was not too deep here, but she knew she would have to be careful not to fall into hidden drifts. Three steps, four steps. The old postman seemed farther away than ever. The only thing she could see clearly about him were his closed eyes. She had the queerest sensation that he was drifting away from her into the snow and however much she moved towards him he would go on moving away from her.

She stared at the space of snow between them that she couldn't seem to get over. And then the snow opened up just like a white misty door, and she forgot all about the postman and dropped her skis and sticks, which fell with scarcely a sound, and stepped over the threshold. And the only thought that struck her was that she had been right about the door but wrong about the keyhole and the tree: Sherry-Sad's door was a Snow Door.

She saw now that the sky wasn't really

pink, and the grass wasn't really blue. The sky was more of a pale violet colour, the way it went sometimes just after the sun had set; and the grass was actually ordinary faded grass, which was reflecting the colour of the sky so that it looked bluish. But the rocks were as she had described them: golden and smooth and almost translucent.

She didn't lick them. She stepped out from between them and walked over the strange-coloured grass. Albert had heard her and turned and stood up as she came towards him.

Barbara wasn't sure what Japanese people looked like, so she didn't know if Albert's slight strangeness was because he looked Japanese. But at any rate she could see that he looked very friendly.

"You came at last!" he said warmly. "I'm glad you did."

Barbara stopped. "Oh," she said, "you speak English – very well."

"And you," he laughed, "you speak Japanese very well!"

"But I'm not speaking Japanese," Barbara said.

"And I'm not speaking English," Albert answered.

Barbara frowned. "Are you teasing me?"

"No," he smiled. "It's because we're in the land at the bottom of the well. Everything's different here – that's why we can understand each other."

"But I don't know about any well," Barbara protested. "Why are you talking about a well?"

"Well, you came down it, so you ought to know," Albert said.

"I didn't come down a well – I came down the path between the rocks. It was quite steep, but it wasn't –"

She had been going to say that the path hadn't been steep enough to call it a well, but she turned round as she spoke to point to where the path came out between the rocks, and there she saw a quite extraordinary thing. The path and the golden rocks were there, sure enough, but they seemed to have tilted in some way, so that they were actually hanging above their heads, just out of reach. She could see the path she had come by, up amongst the hanging rocks, and it was going straight up, exactly like the shaft of a well. "Oh my goodness," was all she could say. And then, "What am I going to do? How shall I get out again?"

Albert smiled again. His teeth were very white. "Now that you've come," he said, "we'll be able to get out together."

"But how?"

"It was the Blue Griffon," he said, very softly. "He made the door and that's how you got down after him. That means he's in his castle now. So I have to attack him in his castle, and rescue you, and then we'll find our way out."

"That's silly," Barbara scoffed. But all the same, when he started striding off in a purposeful manner, she lost no time in following him.

Albert pointed ahead to a line of low cliffs at the far side of a small lake. "That's the castle of the Blue Griffon," he said.

Barbara thought they looked like ordinary cliffs and could see no sign of a castle.

"I've been longing for an adventure," Albert said.

"Have you been here long?" Barbara asked him. "I mean, do you live here?"

Albert didn't answer, though he gave a funny little shrug. "This is going to be a wonderful adventure," he said after a little while.

"I don't know anything about you," Barbara said. "Except your name."

He turned and gave her a beautiful smile, but he still didn't answer her. Barbara began to think he was a little strange.

The lake came nearer. They passed under small clumps of trees with frilled leaves like blue ice. In some of the trees sat the birds with rainbow feathers, unmoving and solemn. It was very quiet and very strange.

They reached the lake, where a small slender boat lay on the shore. The shore was of red and white pebbles, bright as meat laid out in a butcher's window. Albert pushed the boat onto the water and told Barbara to sit in it carefully and not tip it, then he got in behind.

The boat moved off all by itself, and Albert hummed softly, a tune that Barbara almost thought she recognized, but always a little too soft to make out properly. Occasionally he gave a little sniff. By the time they had reached the far shore the humming and the sniffing had begun to annoy her a little.

The boat hit another pebbly beach, and the bottom split open so that red and white stones burst through, like a strange cauliflower that had suddenly sprouted at Barbara's feet. "Look," Albert said in a deep voice, pointing.

Barbara saw a cliff of sandy-coloured rock with bushes growing here and there on its ledges and crevices. "What?" she said.

"The castle of the Blue Griffon," he answered. "This is where I have to rescue you."

"I don't think I need rescuing," she objected.

"Come on," he said, taking her hand and pulling her out of the boat. He hung on to her hand after they were out and starting to make their way up over the pebbles towards the cliff. Barbara wasn't sure she liked this but she didn't try to pull her hand away, just in case she did need some rescuing.

They reached the cliff and climbed onto the first ledge. There was a spindly bush with tiny orange fruit growing on it. "Wait here," Albert whispered. "I'll go on ahead."

Barbara did as she was told. While she was waiting she ate one of the small fruits. It tasted just like an orange, very sweet. Even the skin tasted exactly like candied peel. But eating the fruit made her eyes water, and as she was trying to dry them she noticed that the cliff did seem to be very like a castle after all. It rose in strange terraces and crags, like misshapen battlements and towers.

Albert was spread-eagled against one of its rock walls, peering cautiously round a crag. Barbara decided she had had enough of waiting, and started to follow him.

Chapter Seven

Chapter Seven

When she reached him, he was still in the same position. She thought he might be annoyed with her for disobeying and following him, but he half-smiled at her and laid his finger on his lips. Barbara felt confused about him: he said and did such strange things, but she couldn't deny that she had almost seen a castle when she ate the orange. Maybe he simply knew more than she did about this strange land at the bottom of the well.

"Now!" Albert suddenly yelled so loudly that Barbara jumped and almost toppled forwards over the rocky ledge. Albert leaped out from behind his crag, shouting something which sounded very like "dandara!" She saw now that he had a stick in his hand and he was swishing this through the air or cracking it against the rocks in a very excited fashion, shouting all the time – "Yo! Ha! Whack!

Oocha!" He had a very fierce expression on his face and Barbara even thought he was foaming a little at the mouth, but if he was really fighting he seemed to be fighting empty air. Barbara certainly couldn't see his opponent.

Suddenly he stopped and turned to her. "He's running away up to the tower!" he shouted. "Come on, we've got to get him before he locks himself in! Charge!" And he was off, scrambling and leaping among the crags. Barbara followed more slowly, wishing she had another of the miniature oranges with her just in case it helped her to see what was really going on.

She laboured on up. Although it was very like an ordinary cliff in some ways, she couldn't deny that there seemed to be steps cut in the rock like a real stairway. The cliff – or castle – seemed to be a lot higher when you were in it than when you looked up at it from below. Crags rose all around her like crazy black towers.

She arrived at the biggest one of these to see Albert waiting. She wondered if that meant the Blue Griffon had got into his tower and Albert was locked out. But as soon as she came into sight he suddenly started leaping and whacking again with great fury.

She didn't go any closer, because she had a suspicion that she was in more danger from his flailing stick than the invisible Griffon was. *"Bang! Pow! Yoiks! Hooya!"* Albert screamed and then suddenly sent his stick whirling into the air, where it disappeared over the edge of the cliff. "Oh no!" he howled. "My sword!"

But the loss of his weapon did not dismay him for long. He suddenly did an amazing series of somersaults across the rock, finishing with a dive onto his stomach which Barbara was sure ought to have knocked the breath out of him. He scrambled to his feet, and Barbara saw there was actually a bleeding cut on his now exceedingly dirty face. "Oh, Albert, be careful!" she called.

"You're going to hurt yourself."

"Ya! Bang! Zowf!" he yelled in reply, flinging his arms about and kicking the empty air in front of him so wildly that he lost his balance and fell over onto his back. Barbara was sure he had cracked his head, but undaunted he went rolling over and over, howling and ya-ing, until he reached the very edge of the cliff. There, he lay on his back for a while, kicking his legs wildly up and down and throwing his head from side to side. Suddenly he heaved himself over onto his side, then right over onto his front, screaming "*Blam!* Got you!" and lay still. One arm and one leg were actually hanging over the cliff-edge.

He turned his face to Barbara. "It's all right," he gasped. "I got him."

"Really?" said Barbara, going hesitantly towards him. She felt more confused than ever. She was almost convinced that Albert had been pretending. On the other hand, there was quite a lot of blood coming from the cut on his forehead; so if he had been pretending, he must have been pretending pretty seriously.

"Look," Albert said, pointing over the cliff.

Barbara looked. There was quite a long drop down to the pebbly beach where their burst boat lay. But stare as she might, pebbles were all she could see. Of course she did not know what she was looking for, or if the Blue Griffon were man, bird, beast or monster. She was pretty sure he couldn't just be some coloured pebbles. From this distance, the beach looked pink. "I don't see anything," she said.

"Look, you're not looking," Albert said impatiently. "You can't miss him, he's huge. Down there on the beach."

Barbara looked a while longer. "There's nothing there," she said at length, in a flat voice. "You're just pretending."

"I am not!" he said indignantly, scrambling up. She noticed his knees were bleeding too.

"Yes, you are," she declared. "It's just a

silly boys' game, and now you've made yourself all dirty and cut yourself, and you're just stupid. I don't know why I wanted to come and find you here. I didn't need rescuing."

Albert's expression changed. She could see at once that she had hurt him – and disappointed him too. He got to his feet and walked away from her over to the foot of the tower – or the crag, since it was obvious now that it wasn't a tower. "All right," he said. "I don't care."

Barbara stood contemplating this end to her adventure. "Pleasant Land – the Stupid Land, more like," she muttered. She had hoped for so much more from the magical brother she would find, the mysterious stranger who insisted on being Japanese. And all the time he had just been an ordinary, stupid, messy, noisy, boy. Her eyes pricked: she was starting to cry from sheer disappointment.

But even as the tears formed in her eyes,

she saw the change in the pebbles of the beach down below her. She didn't know if it was because of the tears in her eyes, but the pink of the pebbly beach was fading suddenly, fading to white and then gathering a new colour: faint blue. An outline.

There was a large shape, almost white, mist-blue round the edges, lying across the pink beach. She could not say what it was a shape of – it might have been beast, bird, man or monster – but, "Albert, I can see it now," she said, so softly she hardly even heard herself speak.

Albert was back at her side in an instant. He seemed to have forgiven her completely for not believing him. "Come on," he said, grabbing her hand again. "We've got to go down. He's changing!"

How they got back down the cliff without falling Barbara never knew. Albert held her hand, and she let him: she was too busy thinking about running and not falling. She thought she might have screamed at him to slow down, but if she did he took no notice.

"Oh no," Barbara gasped as they stumbled onto the beach, "he's gone."

"No, it's all right!" Albert called. "He's still changing, look!"

Barbara looked, and this time she saw, without any shadow of doubt.

The great shape had shrunk away, and now there was nothing left of it but a small cone of blue mist. But as they watched, suddenly, out of the mist, a small animal emerged and turned bounding down over the beach.

"Now!" Albert shouted. "Run! Follow!"

And they were running again, pelting down towards the boat after the small streaking shape. What if it disappears in the lake? Barbara thought; but the little animal leaped into the boat, and the boat split into two halves, and as it did so the lake also parted to leave a path through the middle of it between walls of glassy water.

Barbara and Albert never hesitated. Hand in hand, stumbling and gasping, they ran as if their lives depended on it, down, down the path on the bottom of the lake, while the glassy walls towered higher and higher on either side of them.

And then they must have passed the deepest part of the lake, because they started to climb. But although they climbed and climbed – slower now, but still running as hard as they could – the walls of water didn't seem to get any lower, and something made Barbara guess that this land at the bottom of the well was tilting again as it had done before, and they were leaving it behind.

The path rose ahead of them, and now they could see the animal that they were chasing more clearly. A small, long, bluish creature with a long bushy tail and large pricked-up ears. What was it? A fox? There was something fox-like about it, but really it was like different animals: a fox, no – a dog. It was like a dog, and it was also like –

A small dog and a squirrel. It was like a mixture of a Jack Russell terrier and a squirrel.

The animal disappeared from view.

"Nearly there!" Albert gasped. "Don't slow down!"

"I'm not!" Barbara gasped back crossly.

There was nothing. The path stopped, and there was nothing but blackness ahead.

"Don't stop!" Albert yelled.

"No!" Barbara screamed, yanking back at his hand.

He held onto hers tighter. "Jump!" he yelled.

They reached the edge of the nothing. Hand in hand, they jumped.

Chapter Eight

Chapter Eight

Barbara's eyes popped open though she didn't know she had had them shut. It seemed she had returned to the old postman's side; and his eyes, she could see, had just opened as well. There was no sign of Albert or the strange dog-squirrel. The world was white, nothing but white.

"You're right," the postman growled, as if answering something she had said, "they're here." He was looking away from her across the snow. "Well, that's the end of my trip to the Pleasant Land. If it hadn't been for you I could have stayed there."

Miss English and a whole party of people from the village arrived, with blankets and flasks of hot cocoa and a sledge. The old man was lifted, grumbling and protesting, onto the sledge and everyone praised Barbara as if she had done something tremendously brave and heroic.

She felt quite bewildered by it all. She couldn't understand where she had been – or rather, she understood where she had been, but not how she had got there nor how she had got back. She supposed it must have been a kind of dream – and if it had been a dream that must have meant she had fallen asleep, and in that case the old man had probably fallen asleep too and so she certainly hadn't done anything heroic, in fact it was pure luck that her companion was all right.

She also felt depressed. The one person she would have liked to have a little praise from was the old postman, and he grumbled all the way down the hill, mostly about her.

But worse was the thought that she had found her magical story-brother, and then lost him. Worse even than that: as long as she had still been writing her story about the Pleasant Land – making it up, puzzling over the problem of the Japanese boy – it had been a place where she could go and shut out the things in her life that she didn't like, like her mother always drinking sherry and being sad about Uncle Hugh, or like having to go to school in Dundee and not St Syras. But now that she had actually been there, and come back, what was the point of writing the story any more? What was the good of a story compared with the real thing? So she hadn't only lost her magical story-brother; she had lost her magical story-land as well. Everything in her life suddenly seemed very flat, with nothing to look forward to.

The following day, Wednesday, Barbara and Miss English successfully skied to the station at Stratheden and were in time to catch the train. By the day after that the roadmen and the snowploughs had managed to get the road cleared.

As the train crawled through the snowy landscape Barbara wondered if she would ever be able to make up another story. As it clanked over the Tay Bridge and she saw the seals lounging out on the sandbank in the grey water below, she felt a lump coming into her throat because of the way the seals' heads reminded her of the back of Albert's head as he sat on the blue grass of the Pleasant Land.

As more days passed, so did her sadness; but one thing went on puzzling her: the strange little terrier-squirrel that had come out of – or perhaps it had been – the Blue Griffon. It did not take her long to work out that a terrier and a squirrel were the two animals that had played such an important part in the sad story the old postman had told her. If her adventure in the Pleasant Land had been a dream, then that was quite easy to understand, because things from real life always got mixed up in dreams. But she became less and less sure that it had been a dream.

Saturday came, the strangest day of Barbara's life.

The post arrived. "There's a parcel for you,

Barbara!" her mother called.

When Barbara opened the brown paper parcel she found a box of sugared almonds tied with a large red ribbon. When she opened the box there was a letter. It was beautifully written in what her mother called "copperplate handwriting", and it began:

Dear Barbara,

I am afraid I do not know what gift a gentleman should send to a young lady nowadays, so I hope the enclosed sweeties will do.

You saved my life, Barbara, and I shall be ever grateful...

The handwriting was beautiful to look at, but it was a little difficult to read, and Barbara was distracted by the thought of the pretty pink and white and pale-blue sugared almonds. Gently she took a blue one out of its frilled paper nest, sniffed its perfume, brushed it against her lips, and at last popped it into her mouth and sucked. The sugar coating was a little too sweet for her but she liked the salty creaminess of the nut when she got to it; and that was when she let her eyes drift down to the name at the end of the letter.

It was signed "Albert Maxwell".

"Oh my goodness!" she gasped, and almost choked on the nut. She seized the letter again. There was a large paragraph in the middle which she hadn't read yet:

Well my dear I know you don't like to go to school in Dundee; but just think of it: if you hadn't been on your way there that morning we should never have met; and then I should never have heard your story "The Pleasant Land". I know it was supposed to keep me awake but instead it sent me to sleep. Don't worry though, I had a dream that I met my sister Elizabeth again. Also I told her about the dreadful trick I played on her all those years ago and I know she has forgiven me at last. It is all thanks to you, you saved much more than my life.

Perhaps you will visit me one day soon, so that I can tell you the whole exciting story. Yours in gratitude, Albert Maxwell, postie.

"Well," Barbara's mother exclaimed (she had been reading over her shoulder), "you never mentioned any of this before. You must have had quite a chat with Mr Maxwell. And told him a story! Next time I can't get to sleep I'll get you to tell me one too! Perhaps I'll dream I'm with dear Hugh again."

And she went through to the dining-room, where Barbara heard the sound of the sideboard being opened and the sherry glass being taken out. She knew that sound so well: if she kept as still as a mouse she would hear the quiet musical *toonk-toonk-toonk-toonk* as the drink was poured.

But though Barbara kept quieter than any mouse she had known, there was silence instead: a strange sort of waiting silence. And then there was the sound of bottle and glass being put back into the cupboard, and the cupboard door being shut again.

Barbara smiled. She didn't understand, but that didn't seem to matter. Somehow the story of the girl and her imaginary brother had got mixed up with the story of Albert Maxwell and his long-dead sister. And now it seemed another brother and sister were mixed up with it as well: her mother and Uncle Hugh. It was *her* story, and yet it was also much more than her own. "Yes, Mr Maxwell, I'll come and hear it," she said softly; "but perhaps I already know more about it than you think."

BERNARD'S PRIZE
Dick Cate

All Bernard gets from Sports Day is a pain. He never wins a prize. Ozzie Flatt wins every race. *And* he can knock big boys down with a single blow. Perhaps Bernard should stick to painting. Except that the dragon picture he's just done looks amazingly like Ozzie. *And* if Ozzie happens to see it... Read about Bernard's eventful Sports Day in this funny, uplifting story by a prize-winning author.

THE STONE THAT GREW
Enid Richemont

Katie finds the stone in an old box in the loft. It doesn't look like much at first, but then it does something amazing: it grows! Katie thinks it's wonderful. What's more, it's hers and she's not going to share it; it's bad enough having to share Mum with her little stepbrother, Jake. It might even be a way of getting in with Sarah and her gang. Meanwhile the stone continues to grow ... and grow!

MORE WALKER PAPERBACKS
For You to Enjoy

☐ 0-7445-5454-3   *The Boy Who Was a Bear*
by Charles Ashton   £3.99

☐ 0-7445-5250-8   *The Stone that Grew*
by Enid Richemont   £3.99

☐ 0-7445-6034-9   *The Squint*
by Lesley Howarth   £3.99

☐ 0-7445-4759-8   *Bernard's Prize*
by Dick Cate   £3.99

☐ 0-7445-4332-0   *The Amazing Adventures*
of Idle Jack
by Robert Leeson   £3.99

☐ 0-7445-5417-9   *Meet Me by the Steelmen*
by Theresa Tomlinson   £3.99

☐ 0-7445-5203-6   *My Aunty Sal and the*
Mega Sized Moose
by Martin Waddell   £3.99